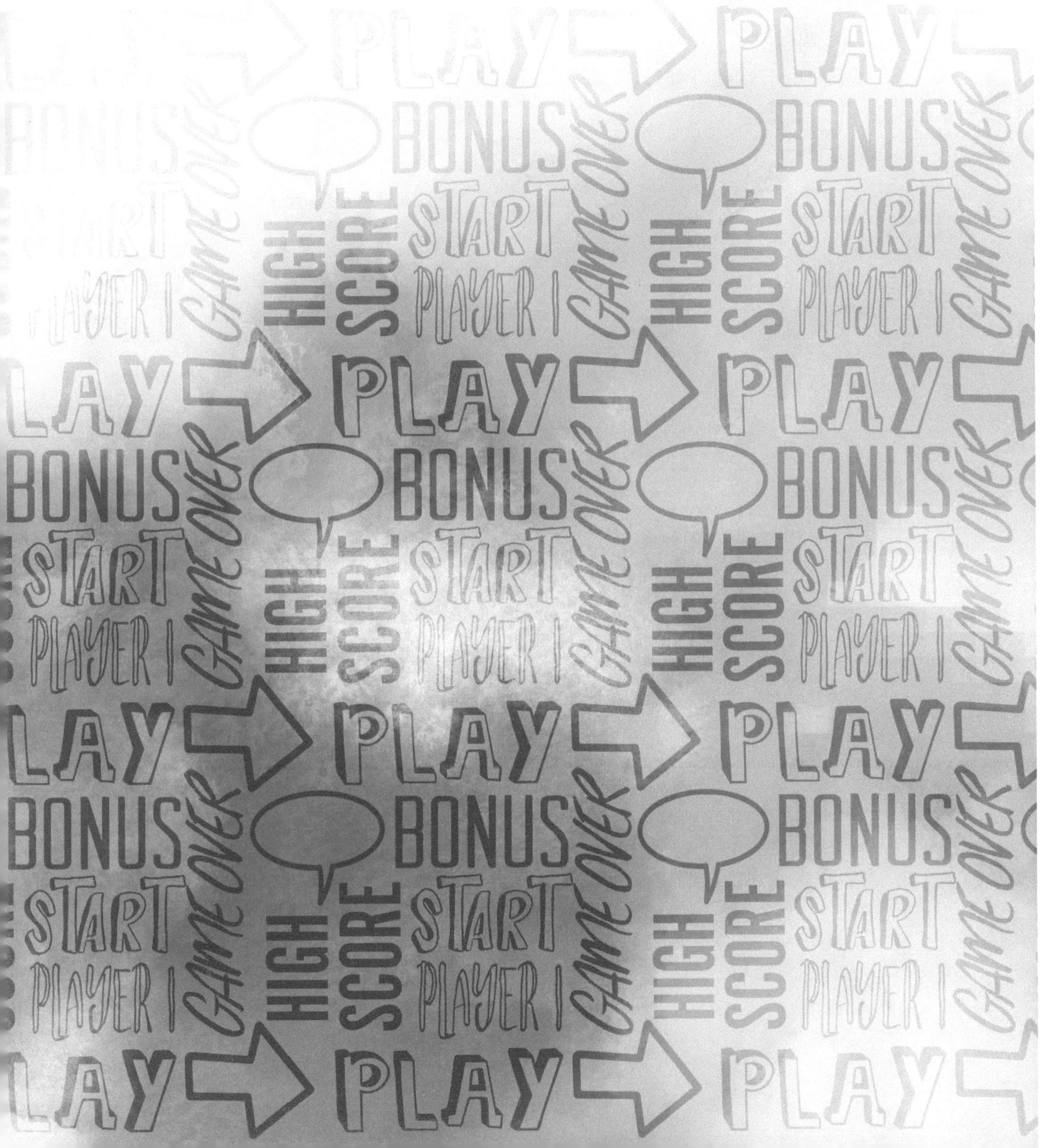
PLAY
BONUS
START
PLAYER 1
GAME OVER
HIGH SCORE

DADDY LET'S PLAY!

Rodney
Freeman, Jr.

First Published - 2021 This edition published 2021
by Preservation LLC, Nashville,
www.reminiscepreservation.com

ISBN 978-1-7367320-2-1 (paperback)
ISBN 978-1-7367320-0-7 (hardcover)
ISBN 978-1-7367320-1-4 (eBook)
Library of Congress Control Number: 2021911222

Book edited by Rebecca Michael

Illustrations and book design copyright © Dorothea Taylor 2021
The illustrations were rendered digitally in Procreate and Photoshop.

This is dedicated to my daughter.
The only way I could keep you a 10-year old
forever. I love you, kiddo!

The best thing in the whole wide world is playing video games with my dad.

Besides me and Mom, Dad also loves our neighborhood. Some days I don't see him until he gets off work from the Community Center.

But when he comes home and before I have to go to bed and say prayers, my dad and I play our favorite video game.

"Daddy, let's play!" I say, thrusting the controller into his hand.

"Milah, we can play one more game before bed.
Let's play the one where I win, Kiddo!"

"No, Daddy. I'm going to win!"

My dad and I always go back and forth, seeing who the best player will be. I'm usually the winner because he doesn't know how to play very well.

In the morning, Dad's usually gone before I wake up. After school, Mom picks me up and I get my homework done, waiting for him to come home. But one day, he doesn't show. Mommy gets a call from my grandma, who sounds upset. Grandma says Daddy will be home after he stops by the hospital. While taking part in a peaceful protest, he started to feel sick.

Mommy says the protest was about people being treated differently because of their skin color. Daddy and the other protesters were asking for equal rights and to all be treated as human beings.

That's why I'm glad I play video games. We can be all different colors like purple and pink, or different shapes like triangles and squares.

"I can't wait for Daddy to come home tonight," I say out loud.

Before I go to bed, I notice Daddy isn't home yet.

"Milah," says Mom, sitting down next to me, "I just received a phone call from the hospital. Daddy is sick and needs to stay there. We won't be able to visit him because of the pandemic."

I don't know what to say. Then, I remember something! When I miss Daddy while he's at work, sometimes he uses his phone so we can play a video game together. *Maybe, just maybe, he has his phone, and we can play,* I think to myself.

"It's time for bed, Milah," Mom says.

"Okay, Mommy," I reply. But before I go to bed, I turn on the game. I'm excited when it loads, and I see all the players with their funny usernames. Then, I see Daddy's avatar, "Bookmanlibrarian." Daddy loves going to the library. He always talks about what it would be like to be a librarian in another life. So he named his avatar "Book Man Librarian."

I feel so happy to see my dad's avatar. In this game, you have to chat with the other players and trade pets to get information. I'm only allowed to chat with friends and family who are approved by my parents.

Yes, Milah. Where am I?"

"You're in the game with me."

"Oh, okay. I must have been out of it."

"Daddy, I'm going to get you out of here. Follow me," I tell him. Luckily, Daddy has played this game with me before, and we should get through. "Dad, watch out!"

"Thanks, Milah. I only have one life, and if I lose it, then it's game over."

"Okay, Daddy. We're almost out of here, but don't get caught—"

"Little girl, what are you doing?" Mommy calls. "Are you on that video game again? Cut it off NOW!" she says with a stinging voice.

"Mommy, I'm playing with Daddy!"

"Milah, we talked about this before. Daddy is in the hospital. He can't play video games right now."

"But I was just playing with him," I plead.

"Go to sleep," she says.

The days drag by. Mommy still looks worried, and Daddy has been gone almost a week.

Finally, one morning, I'm shaken awake. "Milah, Milah! Guess who's at the door!" Mommy says.

My heart races along with my legs to see who it is. I run toward the front door and hear, "Milah, my little rose. Good morning!"

"DADDY!!!" I scream.

My dad picks me up in a big bear hug and then whispers in my ear. "Thank you for showing me the way out."

"I love you, Daddy."

"And I love you too, Kiddo."

"Now, Daddy, let's play!"